MY FRIEND THE ALIEN

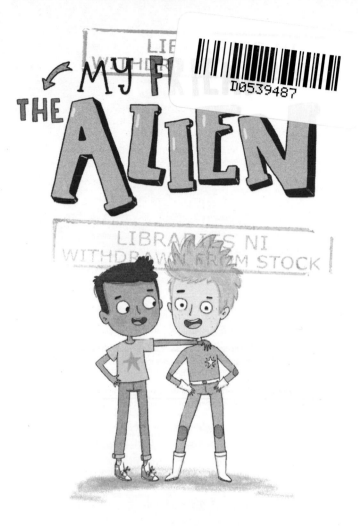

Zanib Mian

Illustrated by Sernur Isik

BLOOMSBURY EDUCATION

LONDON OXFORD NEW YORK NEW DELHI SYDNEY

<u>Day 1</u>

I've landed. Not that you guys
checked up on me or anything, but
I'm fine. The spaceship is fine too,
except for the Filandoo Sperk.

That broke. It wasn't my fault –
I only just looked at it. It's not
important anyway, right?

I landed right where you guys
told me to. In the middle of
nowhere, on some grass. But there
were the things called cows around.

They are animals, I remember from my training. I could see huge puffs of purple gas coming out from their behinds. Methane. Methane is purple. But you know that. By the way, how do you guys know so much about the animals here and almost nothing about the humans?

I'm going to sleep now and will look for the humans tomorrow, to get on with the mission I came here to do:

Find out how humans have feelings.

Day 2

Hey, guys, I'm in a city now, far away from the fields, where there are plenty of humans to watch. I ate my first human food today! It was the most delicious thing I've ever tasted. I got it from a building that was full of all sorts of different things.

It's brown and is called Milk Chocolate with Hazelnut Pieces Sainsbury's Taste the Difference.

Long name, but tastes awesome. I think I'll be happy if I find nothing else to eat here on Earth other than Milk Chocolate with Hazelnut Pieces Sainsbury's Taste the Difference.

I made my first observation when I was inside that building. Humans release methane too. Though not as much as cows. The place was full of purple gas, which the humans released as they pushed around these metal cages and put things into them. Some of them shouted a lot at the little humans, who seemed to want to put things in the metal cage that the big ones didn't want there.

Then a couple of the little ones
started making shrieking noises and
had water coming out of their eyes.
I guess those are feelings; one type
of feelings.

I haven't seen the big ones showing many yet. Well, they haven't made any of the shrieking noises.

As instructed, I will use the thing called Google to find out more about feelings.

By the way, nobody noticed me. Nobody thought I was strange.

They don't know I'm not from around here, because I look just like them.

Day 3

Google says these guys have a gazillion different kinds of feelings. And they can be so soppy, it's unbelievable. The yuckiest one I read about was LOVE. Ewww.

I need to get out there, to places where there are lots of humans, to find out how these feelings happen.

In the afternoon, I hopped on a bus, which is an extra-long vehicle where humans sit and stand very close together.

So close that I learned that some humans have not very nice smells coming from them. A nasty gas comes from their mouths and stinky water trickles from their armpits, and then obviously there is the methane. I did not enjoy being on that bus.

Then I went to the park, where some of them were running around (extremely slowly) and some were walking with the little humans. I thought I'd run too, but some of them started looking at me and pointing, so I stopped. At the place

I sat down, one human was showing its tiny little dog to another human. I guess it was a baby dog, but I forget the name for those.

The human was saying, "Awww, isn't he just the most adorable thing?" And her face was changing and she kept putting her hand on her heart.

I felt nothing. It's just a creature. What's the big deal? But I think it might be something to do with the love feeling that this human was suffering from. Then she said, "He's so fluffy and cute, I just want to eat him."

So I found out that feelings can happen by looking at things and humans want to eat things they think are cute. I got a bit closer to see how they smell, but the little dog started going crazy and showing me its teeth. It wasn't speaking human, but it was pretty clear it wanted to eat ME. So I ran and it ran after me. It was nowhere near as fast as me, but to be safe, I dropped to the floor and became invisible. The dog ran on, confused.

Sheesh, what just happened there? It seems even the animals here have feelings. I'm not sure I can complete this mission by myself. It's colossal! Also, I haven't heard a squeak out of you guys since I got here. Are you glad to be rid of me?

Day 4

I made friends with one of the humans today. Yes, yes, I know I am breaking the rules. I'm only supposed to look at them and not touch, blah, blah, blah. But it spoke to ME. And anyway, I need help. I can't complete this mission by myself. It's too much work for one Zerglid.

It happened in one of those buildings full of all the things, where humans go to get the stuff they want. I was walking past the books and magazines – they have those just like we do! I saw one called

'Aliens from Outer Space'. *Hey, that
must be about us!* I thought, and then
I couldn't believe what I saw. They
had drawn us green, with antennae!
And we had no clothes on. Do
they think we have no shame? And
green? Who told them we are green?

Basically, they think we're pretty ugly and slimy-looking.

So I was standing there, holding the book, gaping and gasping with disbelief, when the human came up to me. It was a medium-sized one, not big and not small and tiny.

And it said, "Aliens are cool, right? But pretty ugly."

So I said, "No we're not!"

The human smiled and said, "*We?* Do you mean you *are* one or something?"

And I said, "Yes and I'm not ugly. I look the same as you, actually."

The human laughed and said, "You're funny. My name's Jibreel. I'm named after an angel."

So I said, "My name, is Maxx. I don't know what I'm named after, but it's probably an alien."

The human laughed again. His eyes were sparkly when he laughed and his face looked nice. Better than humans look when they're shrieking. Then he asked me if I'm going to the 'All Things Alien' exhibition in the library. I said of course I am, because I love aliens and he said he'll see me there at lunchtime tomorrow.

I think I'll learn a lot from Jibreel.

When I walked out of the building, I saw two male humans fighting about which one could put their vehicle in a space on the road. I guess they haven't learned to zap shrink their vehicles to save space, like we do. This was an interesting thing to watch because it was the first time I saw the anger feeling.

I didn't know humans can change colour, but it happens when they get angry – both of these humans were going red! One of them threw their cup of brown liquid at the other one's vehicle, which made him jump out and thump on the window of the first one's vehicle. It ended up with both of them punching each other in their red faces, and they didn't stop until a short, wrinkly human that moves extra slowly came and started whacking them both with her handbag.

So basically feelings are flying around everywhere and humans don't seem to be able to control them. And did I mention, they think we are *green*?

Day 5

Today I met Jibreel at the library for the
All Things Alien exhibition. You're not
going to believe this… they think we
have been *stealing* humans from Earth,
just zapping them up whenever we feel
like it, to experiment on. The whole
exhibition was a complete abomination.

I found Jibreel at the 'Guess
What Aliens Smell Like' stall. Yes,
you read that right. *They're* the
smelly ones, with their methane and
their stinky armpit water and bad
mouth gas. At the stall, they had
seven pots of smells. Six of them
were horrible and only one smelled
nice. It was labelled 'bubble gum'.

I was quite impressed that Jibreel voted for the bubble gum, because forty-three other people voted for the really yucky one called 'pond slime'.

"I don't actually smell of anything," I told Jibreel. "Aliens have no smell. And no feelings."

Jibreel laughed and sniffed me. "Actually, you smell just like chocolate."

"What? What's chocolate? I don't smell of chocolate!"

"What's chocolate?" Jibreel laughed again. This human laughs a lot. "You smell very strongly of chocolate."

I patted myself where Jibreel had sniffed, and found my half-eaten Milk Chocolate with Hazelnut Pieces Sainsbury's Taste the Difference.

"Ah, yes. That. That's my favourite Earth food."

Jibreel slapped his knee and laughed a lot more. "You're really funny, Maxx. I like you," he said and grabbed my arm. "Let's get the lift upstairs. Come on, there's lots to see!"

We walked through a sea of balloons shaped like green aliens with antennae. Sheesh, these humans really need to have more

of an imagination. Or better space
scientists.

But round the corner, Jibreel
saw something that made his face
change completely. It didn't look like
it does when he's laughing. It went a
different colour, but not red like the
angry humans. It just looked like his
normal colour was fading.

I poked him. "Jibreel? Jibreel? Are you suffering from a feeling?"

He looked like he wasn't listening and as if he was trying to hide. So I poked him again and finally he said, "Yes… those boys are from my school and let's just say they're trouble."

"So what was the feeling you were having?" I asked, because this was a learning opportunity for me and for all Zerglids, thanks to me.

"Worried. Anxious. Scared," said Jibreel. "What a funny question, Maxx. You sound like one of those adults at school who take you into a room to talk about life and feelings."

"Wow, you have humans that do that? Is it because they don't understand what feelings are, either?"

"No, it's because they want to help."

This was confusing, but I didn't have time to ask more because we had to run away from the trouble.

When we ran, I ran like a normal alien and saw that Jibreel had got left behind. When he caught up, he said, "What on earth? How did you do that? Do you have rocket shoes or something?"

"Do what?" I asked.

"Run so fast!"

"It's how I run," I said. "Sixty miles per hour, like everyone else."

"Er, everyone else doesn't run at sixty miles per hour. Usain Bolt is the fastest human on Earth and even he can only run at like thirty miles per hour."

"Yes, but I'm not human," I said once again. And now I understand why everyone was staring at me in the park.

"Ha ha, you're going to stick to your alien story are you?" grinned Jibreel. And he took out a wrapped object and gave it to me.

I opened the wrapper. It contained brown food. I took a bite, and oh my taste buds! I guess all

wrapped-up brown food must be
chocolate.

Jibreel looked very happy to see
me eating. His eyes were sparkly
again. He had forgotten all about
the trouble.

I snapped off a piece of the
chocolate and gave it to him. He
took it happily. As if it hadn't been
his in the first place. He ate the

chocolate slowly, in tiny bits. My brother would never have given me his whole tribus, which I think is the tastiest thing we have on Zerg.

"Let's go check out the alien costumes downstairs," said Jibreel, and again he took my hand and started running. This time it was happy running. Jibreel was displaying all sorts of feelings, one after the other.

We went through a door and then something crazy happened. The floor became a funny shape! Like downwards zigzags. Jibreel kept on without stopping, just walking on them like it was nothing. But not me. I fell over my feet on the

zigzags and went head first right to
the bottom of them, banging my
head and my bottom lots of times on
the way.

"Oh my God," said Jibreel. "Are
you OK? Are you OK?"

I jumped up. "Completely fine. Our bodies are used to going through worse than that. It was just a surprise."

Jibreel didn't seem to believe me. He was grabbing my arms and checking them over. "But you fell down the stairs! All the stairs!"

"Is that what you call them? They're really annoying, what are they for?"

"For going up and down, you crazy thing," said Jibreel and he put his arms round me and his cheek against my cheek and stayed there. "Hugs always make people better."

Hugs. You guys, hugs are cool. They made me forget all about the annoying zigzags.

P.S. When I return, I want a medal that says: 'Colossal Mission Complete'.

Day 8

Sorry! I know I haven't reported back for a few days, and I'm supposed to do it every day, but I've just been so busy hanging out with Jibreel. And anyway, I still haven't heard from you guys.

We've done all sorts of cool things. We went to the cinema to see *Big Hero 6*. There are some really great hugs in that movie. I'll bring a copy home to teach everyone how to do them.

I also discovered more Earth food that I like – popcorn, waffles and pizza.

And Jibreel has finally believed me about being an alien.

When we were queuing up to
leave the cinema, those nasty boys
from Jibreel's school came up behind
us. Jibreel immediately stopped
moving. He went all quiet and still
as a statue.

"Oh look, it's the alien!" said one of the boys.

"Stinky, smelly alien. Go back to where you came from!" snarled another.

What? How do they know I'm an alien? I was thinking.

And Jibreel was shrinking further and further into himself.

One of the boys released the purple gas and they all started holding their noses and pointing at each other to say who did it. Then they started throwing popcorn at us. Quite a lot of it. One bit hit me right in the eye, so I thought, *Right, that's enough of that*, and I took Jibreel's hand and made both of us invisible.

"What? Where did they go? Where did they go?" said the confused boys.

"They must have run off," one of them decided.

"It looked like they just disappeared," said another.

"Weird aliens," added the third.

I held my finger to my lips to tell Jibreel to stay quiet. He looked stunned. Then just for fun, I flicked one of the boys' ears.

He clapped his hand over it immediately.

"Who did that?" he demanded.

While they were arguing, we slid out the door and ran away. We ran out into the car park and then I made us both visible again. I let go of Jibreel, who had a look of mild panic mixed with thrill in his eyes.

"What on earth just happened, Maxx?"

"Not Earth. Well, I mean it's not from Earth. The invisibility thing. It's from Zerg."

"Zerg?"

"Yes, Zerg. Where I come from. I keep telling you – I'm an alien."

Jibreel started laughing. But it wasn't like the laughs he had done before when he was having the happy feelings. This was a laugh that made him look crazy. It was as if he had to laugh OR faint in disbelief. I guess it must be hard for a human to understand that aliens look like me and not like those ugly green things with antennae that they've been dreaming up.

"I TOLD you the day we met."

"I thought you were kidding!" said Jibreel, finally looking at me.

He poked me in the arm and watched carefully to see what would happen. "What are you made of?"

"I don't know. Stuff. What are YOU made of?" I said, poking him back.

That made him laugh. The real kind of laugh.

"How did those boys know I'm an alien?" I asked.

"They didn't… they don't. They call ME alien."

"What? Are you an alien too? Then why do you run so *slowly*, and why do you release the purple gas? Which planet are you from?"

"Not that kind of alien... They call me alien because I'm not from this country... I'm a refugee."

"A refugee?"

"Yes. There was a horrible war in my country, so I had to come and live here."

"But you're still a human? From Earth?"

"Of course!"

"So why do they call you alien?"

"I don't know... I guess cos they think I'm different to them." Jibreel couldn't even hold his shoulders up when he said this. Nor his head, which was flopped towards the ground. "They don't like me because I come from somewhere else..."

Guys, I don't know what it was but I felt a speck. A teeny tiny speck of something new in my body. It was warm, like the toasted waffles I had eaten earlier.

Day 12

Yup. Since you guys aren't EVEN BOTHERING to respond to me, I am not going to bother reporting every day.

So let's see. What have I been up to…?

Mostly, I've been hanging out with Jibreel in the park.

Jibreel is interesting. Did you know, in his country, before he came here, he won an award for making some high-tech science thing in his spare time. He reminds me of you guys, and by that I mean geeky with a touch of cool, or just geeky, which is the new cool anyway, so…

Jibreel has been asking me lots of questions about people from Zerg. The first thing he wanted to know was what other 'powers' I have.

"You know," he said, with a mouth full of cheese puffs – a delicious orange food, which are so light, it hardly feels like you're holding them. "You can make yourself invisible and run really fast. What else can you do?"

"I can make people do things just by thinking about it," I said.

"NO WAY! Like what?"

"Anything I want," I said.

"Make me do something!"

"OK."

So I made him spit out his cheese puffs all over the park bench.

Then I made him hop on one leg for thirty-four seconds.

"Oh my God. That's awesome!" Jibreel was ecstatic. "Why haven't we been having FUN with it?"

"What do you mean?"

"Well, you can make people do funny things!"

"What do humans find funny?" I asked, making notes for my mission as Jibreel listed them.

THINGS THAT HUMANS FIND FUNNY:

Farting (purple gas)	Falling over
Burping (blue gas)	Wetting themselves
Snot	Poo jokes

"If I made those nasty boys at your school do those things," I asked Jibreel, "would people laugh at them and would that give you a happy feeling?"

Jibreel put on a thinking face. To think, he squashes his eyebrows together and turns his eyeballs left and upwards. I've noticed that humans sometimes take a long time to think, and even then they don't always have answers.

Finally, Jibreel said, "It would be really funny," (and he giggled while he said that) "but it's a mean thing to do and it would make them feel sad for a long time. I don't like making people feel sad."

"Sheesh, Jibreel, you're sounding really cheesy you know. Are all humans as cheesy as you?" I teased.

Jibreel blushed pink. "But it's true. Two wrongs don't make a right."

I didn't know what to say to something like that, so I emptied the bag of cheese puffs on my head and Jibreel laughed.

Day 14

Today, when I went to meet Jibreel in the park, I didn't find him smiling at the ducks or petting someone's dog. I found him lying on the grass with water rolling down his cheeks.

"Jibreel?" I poked him. I don't know why, but poking is the first thing I do whenever Jibreel is suffering from a feeling.

"Yeah." He sniffed and wiped the water with the back of his hand.

"Feelings again?" I asked, and then I showed off everything I had learned so far. "Sad feelings. Opposite of happy. Crying?"

"Yes," he hiccupped.

"Why is this happening?" I said. "Did you fall down the zigzags?"

"No."

"What then?"

"I miss my mum."

"Where is she?"

"She couldn't escape here with me and my brother. She's still in my country and I worry about her all the time. Even when I'm trying to have fun."

"Y-you… You…" Guys, that's all I could say. Remember I told you about the warm speck I felt in my body. Well, it was a bigger warm thing now, more like a tennis ball, and I was horrified to discover that it might be a *feeling*.

I had a feeling! A feeling that was sad for Jibreel. Oh my God, he couldn't be with his mum and it was making him spill water from his eyes and lie on the grass and completely ignore the ducks.

"I miss her hugs," he burst out.

And I wasn't expecting this, but then I made him sit up and I gave him a hug, which made the warm thing in me grow to at least basketball size.

Whoa. Guys, I'm becoming like an Earth creature. I couldn't get rid of my feeling. I told it to go away, but it just stayed there being warm inside me.

Then Jibreel reached for his rucksack and fished out a piece of paper.

"I'm usually OK, until something like this happens," he said.

The hug must have worked because the water had stopped rolling down his cheeks. All that was left was a tiny drop of snot that had escaped his nose.

I looked at the paper. It was human writing. It said:

Hello Alien,

Nobody likes you. Go back home where there might be a tiny chance you could have a friend.

P.S. Are you an orphan too?

When I read it, I had ANOTHER feeling. It was like now one had got inside me, they had all been let loose. This feeling was anger and it was making me feel very hot at the top of my head.

I thought of the angry red humans from the other day.

"Am I changing colour, Jibreel? Am I going red?" I asked.

"Er, yes, actually I think you are a bit!" said a surprised Jibreel.

I stood up and tried to run away from the feelings. But they wouldn't leave.

"What if there's something in your water here on Earth?" I panted.

Well, that's the only reasonable explanation I could think of. I was feeling-free when I arrived. Then I ate their food, drank their water and breathed their air, so the feelings must have come from one of those.

Poor humans, they've had all three of those things since they were born. No wonder their feelings are all over the place.

Day 15

The feelings have gone away. But I woke up with an idea that I just couldn't get rid of.

I made myself invisible and followed Jibreel to school. I almost missed the bus he got on, because the driver shut the door and started driving off, so I had to make him reverse and open the door again. Everyone on the bus was looking at each other, wondering what was going on. Even the driver was looking at his hands and shaking his head.

When we got to school, I slipped
into Jibreel's classroom, right behind
him, and watched the rest of the kids
come in, chewing their bubble gum
and chatting about their favourite
TV shows. The teacher wasn't there
yet. Then the nasty boys came in
together, all three of them. Most
of the other kids grew quiet when
they came in. I think those boys

scare everyone. They stood near the teacher's desk, talking in loud voices, as if they were in charge.

I didn't waste any time. I made one of them release the noisiest, most stinky purple gas ever. Then as the whole class were coughing and holding their noses, I made the

second one do twelve loud burps in one go. Then I made the third one sneeze, and a load of snot flew out of his nose and down towards his mouth in uncontrollable pint-sized portions. While at the same time, the first boy let off another whopper of a bottom burp that propelled him at least two metres forward to his desk, which he crawled underneath and hid with shame.

The room of kids was now out of control in complete ecstatic joy at this humiliating set of circumstances that their not-so-favourite classmates had suffered.

But not Jibreel. Jibreel wasn't laughing. He was going a bit red in the face and looking around as if he was trying to find someone.

"MAXXXXXXXX!" he finally blurted.

Oh yikes! He knew it was me. Of course he knew it was me.

"Come to the toilets now!" he shouted to thin air. Thankfully all the other kids were too busy pointing and laughing at the series of unfortunate bodily functions the three boys had had, to notice Jibreel speaking to nobody.

I followed him to the toilets and made myself visible.

"Why did you do that?" gasped Jibreel.

"Didn't you think it was funny?"

"I did… and I didn't. I didn't laugh!" Jibreel spoke to me, but it looked like he was telling himself. "The point is, it was *not* nice."

"Er, it wasn't supposed to be *nice*."

Jibreel gave me the one-eyebrow-raised look, which I have discovered means he's not impressed, so I said, "I wonder what kind of feelings they're having now."

"They're probably feeling ashamed and humiliated. Maybe even worried, about what's going to happen next."

"Worried? Which one is that?"

"It's when you have a problem and you keep thinking about what might happen."

"Oh… How does it feel when you have a worry?"

"You don't have a worry, you just worry," laughed Jibreel. "Well, sometimes when I'm worried my tummy hurts."

And just then my tummy started hurting, right in the middle where my Zerg button is. I didn't know what it was before, because I'm not supposed to *have* feelings, but I have had a worry for a while now.

I held my tummy and told Jibreel, "I have a worry. I have a worry because I am thinking the Filandoo Sperk on my spaceship might have been important after all, and maybe that's why I haven't heard from the guys back home. And what if I never get to go home because the spaceship isn't working?"

"Maxx, it's going to be OK," said Jibreel. "Breathe in and out, like this. It's something I do, when I remember I'm not going home."

He was so brave and such a good friend that my basketball exploded into a warm and mushy hot-air balloon

right inside my chest. I took Jibreel and
gave him a *Big Hero* 6 style hug.

We agreed to meet after school
so I can tell him more about the
Filandoo Sperk.

Day 15 (later)

So now you guys know. I am
WORRIED that I haven't heard
from you. Couldn't you find some
other way to get in touch? Don't
worry, though, we're working on it.
Oh, I forgot, you don't have feelings,
so you can't worry. You don't know
how lucky you are – feelings are
hard. I wonder if I will still have
feelings when I get back to Zerg. I
hope I do. What? It may be hard,
but they feel nice.

I met with Jibreel again in
the park. We could see the three

nasty boys nearby, but we knew
they wouldn't be bothering anyone
today. We also saw a baby dog,
and I thought it was so fluffy and
cute, I wanted to eat it. WHAT IS
HAPPENING TO ME?

Anyway, we ate some Chocolate
with Hazelnut Pieces Sainsbury's
Taste the Difference and I told
Jibreel all about the spaceship and
the broken bit that I thought wasn't
important. He said that maybe he
can help, because the science thing
he made in his country, which won
a prize, meant that he had to learn a
lot of physics and electrical stuff.

So I took Jibreel to the spaceship.
Yes, yes, I know, I'm not supposed to
let humans see my ship, blah, blah,
blah, but this is Jibreel and anyway
what else am I supposed to do?

We had to walk all the way to
the field where the cows are, because
Jibreel can't keep up when I run.
I don't know what they had been

eating, but when we got there, the field was misty with purple gas.

We took off the camouflage blanket and went inside.

Jibreel was amazed by what he saw. "I can't believe it's a real-life alien spaceship!"

He kept asking questions about everything!

"What does this button do?"

"How fast does it go?"

"How did you learn to drive it?"

"Where have you been in it?"

"What does *this* button do?"

"Do you have a button that blasts your seat into space?"

All good questions, but I was eager to get him started on the Filandoo Sperk. I shoved it in his hands and looked at him with flying-saucer eyes.

"Well? Can you fix it?"

"Maxx, my friend, I might just be able to. But I need to get it home where my tools are."

So we shoved it in his backpack and off we went.

Day 18

CODE RED. CODE RED. MISSING SPACESHIP. HELP ME!

OK, so I'm sorry I haven't sent a report in a few days, but first of all, it feels funny talking so much when nothing is coming back, and second, I've been busy watching Jibreel be smarter than you guys and actually fixing the Filandoo Sperk! But when we went back to the spaceship, IT WASN'T THERE.

IT ISN'T THERE.

I looked within a six-hundred-metre radius, just in case a couple of

cows might have managed to bump it along with their rear ends, but it really is missing and I don't even know HOW!

Guys, my stomach really hurts now. Please, please help.

Day 19

Checked again for the spaceship.
Still not there. Stomach still hurting.
Feelings levels rising.

Day 20

Checked again for the spaceship.
Still not there. Stomach still hurting.
Feelings levels rising.

Day 21

Checked again for the spaceship.
Still not there. Stomach still hurting.
Feelings levels rising.

Day 21 (Zerg) 4.52 p.m.

COME IN, MAXX. COME IN,
MAXX. YOUR SPACESHIP
HAS JUST LANDED ON ZERG
WITH THE THREEE NASTY-
LOOKING HUMAN BOYS IN IT.
THEY SAY THEY FOLLOWED
YOU AND JIBREEL FROM
THE PARK, BECAUSE THEY
WERE SUSPICIOUS AFTER
THE CLASSROOM INCIDENT
(WHICH WAS AGAINST
PROTOCOL MIGHT WE ADD).
THEY SAW YOU UNVEIL THE
SPACESHIP AND DECIDED TO

POKE AROUND WHEN YOU
LEFT. THEY POKED ONE GREY
BUTTON TOO MANY, SO THE
SHIP WENT INTO AUTOPILOT
BACK TO ORIGIN. THE BOYS
ARE NOT DOING WELL.
THANKS TO YOUR MISSION
AND REPORTS, WE NOW KNOW
THEY ARE 'CRYING', PROBABLY
BECAUSE THEY ARE WORRIED
AND MAYBE THEIR STOMACHS
HURT? WE ARE SENDING THEM
BACK IMMEDIATELY WITH THE
FIRST AVAILABLE ZERG PILOT,
WHO WILL BE MAKING A
SMALL DETOUR ON THE WAY.

Day 21 (Earth) 4.55 p.m.

WOW, guys, we can hear you through the Filandoo Sperk! I guess you must be able to connect to it now that you have the spaceship! It feels so good to hear your voices but I CAN'T BELIEVE what you're saying! Jibreel is here too and he thinks it's nuts. We both think it's nuts!

Day 21 (Zerg) 4.57 p.m.

YOU'LL BE HOME SOON,
MAXX. DON'T DO THIS NEW
TRICK YOU'VE LEARNED, THE
WORRYING.

Day 21 (Zerg) 6 p.m.

SHIP LAUNCHED. EXPECT IT
ON DAY TWENTY-SEVEN AT
6 P.M.

Day 27 6 p.m.

OK, guys, it's day twenty-seven. I'm waiting here with Jibreel. He's really excited. He has lost the ability to stand still.

Ah, right on time, I see the ship. It's preparing to land.

"Stand back, Jibreel. It will be way too windy for your human abilities in that spot."

"OK! I'm just so excited to see it land!"

Ship has landed successfully.

Ship door is opening.

Zerg pilot is coming out, followed by three boys, who er, don't look so nasty any more.

Er, three boys have run up to us and given Jibreel and me hugs, and said they're glad to see us (so glad). O-K.

Wait, one more human is coming off the ship… What? Did she go with the boys?

What? Jibreel has just seen her and has broken down crying. He's wrapped himself around her. She is crying too.

"My son, my son," she is saying.

Wait, guys, did you find his mum? You didn't… *That* was the detour…? Wow. I mean, wow. Are you sure you guys don't have feelings too? Ouch, guys, I'm having too many feelings. My eyes are watering. Everyone's eyes are watering, but it's happy water.

Day 35

10 a.m. Earth: Come in, Maxx, come in, Maxx, this is Jibreel speaking. Have you reached Zerg safely?

10.01 a.m. Zerg: I know it's Jibreel speaking, because no other human has a way of contacting us! Yes! I reached Zerg safely. I've been doing lots of interviews here about Earth life! What have you been up to?

10.03 a.m. Earth: I've been enjoying Mum's hugs. I can't believe she's with me again. Sometimes, I get up in the middle of the night just to check. Oh, and those three boys have never called me alien again. Oh, and I've started a social media campaign to improve the image of aliens!

10.05 a.m. Zerg: Ha ha, that's awesome, Jibreel. I can't wait to come back to Earth for another mission. See you soon!

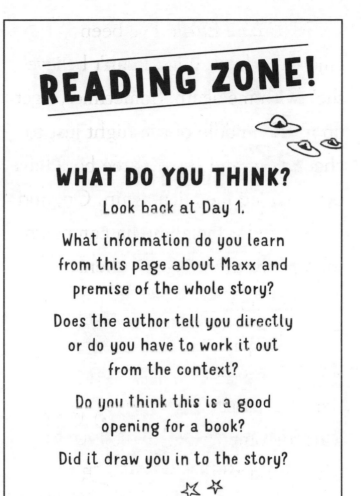

READING ZONE!

WHAT DO YOU THINK?

Look back at Day 1.

What information do you learn from this page about Maxx and premise of the whole story?

Does the author tell you directly or do you have to work it out from the context?

Do you think this is a good opening for a book?

Did it draw you in to the story?

READING ZONE!

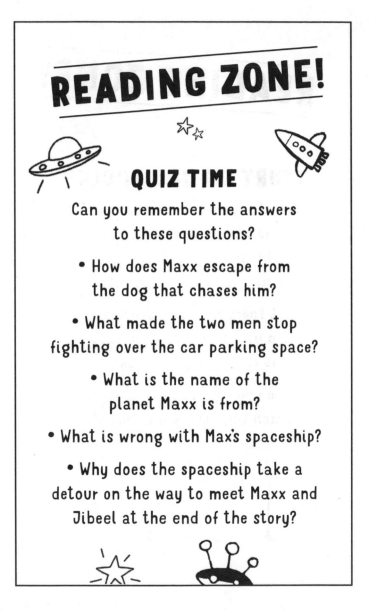

QUIZ TIME

Can you remember the answers
to these questions?

• How does Maxx escape from
the dog that chases him?

• What made the two men stop
fighting over the car parking space?

• What is the name of the
planet Maxx is from?

• What is wrong with Max's spaceship?

• Why does the spaceship take a
detour on the way to meet Maxx and
Jibeel at the end of the story?

READING ZONE!

STORYTELLING TOOLKIT

This story uses the messages that Maxx is writing to his home planet, and the messages the people there write back to tell the story.

What tools has the author used to help us (the reader) understand who is sending the messages?

Have you ever read another book which tells the story this way?

READING ZONE!

GET CREATIVE

In his messages back home, Max describes some ordinary things in lots of detail, like the way he talks about the bus on page 4.

Try choosing an activity you do or something you eat or drink and write an explanation of it as if you are Maxx writing home.

Think about what he would see or experience to help you write in the style of Maxx!